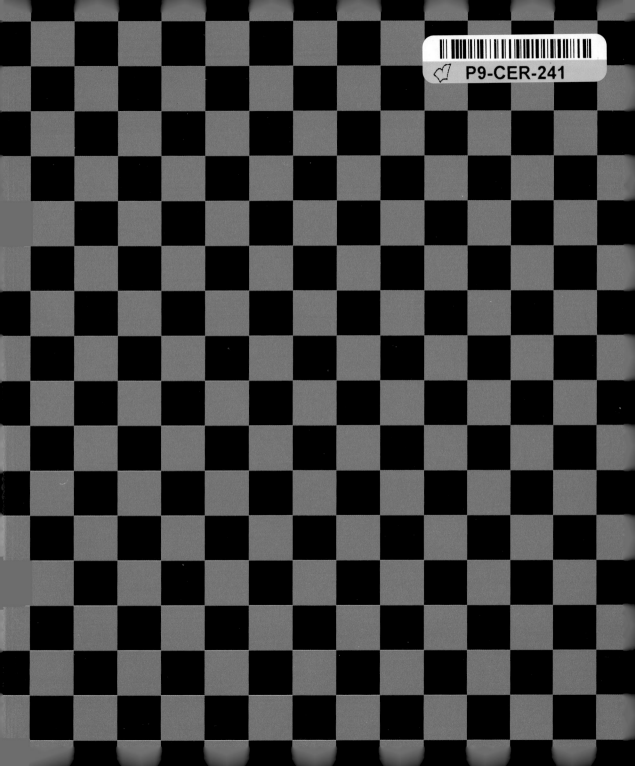

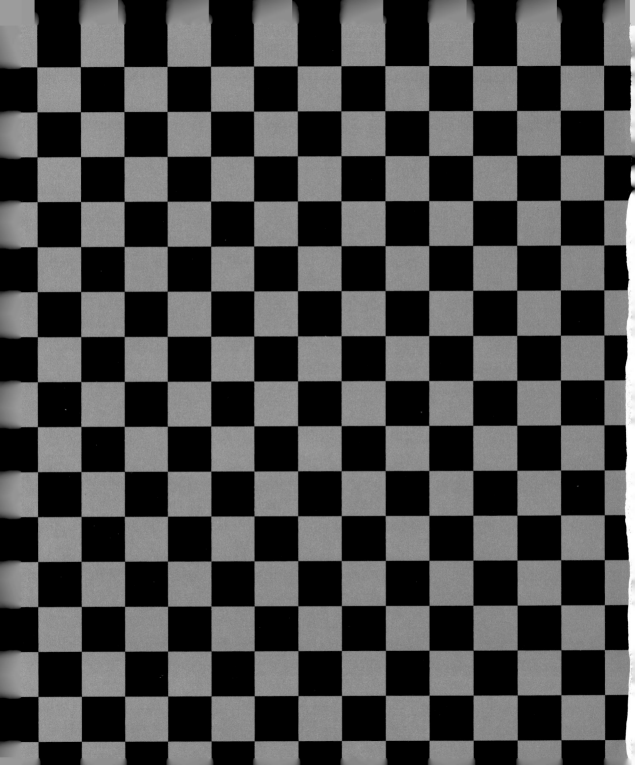

FOOD TALES

FOOD TALES

A Literary Menu of Mouthwatering Masterpieces

WITH PHOTOGRAPHS BY Laurie Rubin

INTRODUCTION BY MIMI SHERATON

VIKING
STUDIO
BOOKS

For Bruce and Cole, the lights of my life.

VIKING STUDIO BOOKS

Published by the Penguin Group
Viking Penguin, a division of Penguin Books USA Inc., 375 Hudson Street,
New York, New York 10014, U.S.A.
Penguin Books Ltd, 27 Wrights Lane, London W8 5TZ, England
Penguin Books Australia Ltd, Ringwood, Victoria, Australia
Penguin Books Canada Ltd, 10 Alcorn Avenue, Suite 300,
Toronto, Ontario, Canada M4V 3B2
Penguin Books (N.Z.) Ltd, 182–190 Wairau Road, Auckland 10, New Zealand

Penguin Books Ltd, Registered Offices: Harmondsworth, Middlesex, England

First published in 1992 by Viking Penguin, a division of Penguin Books USA Inc.

1 3 5 7 9 10 8 6 4 2

Copyright © Fly Productions, 1992
Photographs copyright © Laurie Rubin, 1992
Introduction copyright © Mimi Sheraton, 1992
All rights reserved

Grateful acknowledgment is made for permission to reprint the following
copyrighted works:

"Yesterday's Sweetmeats" by Robert Benchley. Reprinted by permission of Liberty Library Cor-
poration from *Liberty Magazine.* Copyright © 1932 Liberty Publishing Corp.
"The Luncheon" by W. Somerset Maugham. By permission of A. P. Watt Limited on behalf of
the Royal Literary Fund.
"The Man Who Loved to Eat" by William Maxwell. By permission of Wylie, Aitken & Stone, Inc.
"The Spoiled Cake" by Jules Renard, translated by Ralph Manheim from *French Stories and
Tales* by Stanley Geist, editor. Copyright 1954 by Alfred A. Knopf, Inc. and renewed 1982
by Stanley Geist. Reprinted by permission of the publisher.
"Tortillas and Beans" from *Tortilla Flat* by John Steinbeck. Copyright 1935, renewed © 1963
by John Steinbeck. Used by permission of Viking Penguin, a division of Penguin Books
USA Inc.
"The Power of Cookery" from *Kingdoms of Elfin* by Sylvia Townsend Warner. By permission
of Chatto & Windus as Executors fo the Estate of Sylvia Townsend Warner.
"His Father's Earth" from *The Web and the Rock* by Thomas Wolfe. Copyright 1937, 1938,
1939 by Maxwell Perkins as Executor, renewed 1967 by Paul Gitlin, C.T.A., Administra-
tor of the Estate of Thomas Wolfe.

LIBRARY OF CONGRESS CATALOGING IN PUBLICATION DATA
Food tales: a literary menu of mouthwatering masterpieces / with photographs
by Laurie Rubin.
p. cm.
ISBN 0–670–84046–7
1. Short stories. 2. Food — Fiction. I. Rubin, Laurie.
PN6120.95.F6F6 1992
808.83'1 — dc20   91–33843

Printed in Japan

Special thanks to Samuel Mitnick for his
valuable editorial contribution.

ACKNOWLEDGMENTS

I wish to thank Linda and Larry, my earliest victims, for patiently indulging me. My parents, Ron and Deborah, for all those delayed dinners and for fixing what was broken. Betty and Leslie for always searching for the most perfect obscure objects. Donna and Dave for making it possible for me to get home before midnight. Rita and Esther for putting this book together. Rich and Herb for advice and guidance, and for keeping me out of trouble. And Randy, without whom I might still be a waitress.

CONTENTS

INTRODUCTION BY

MIMI SHERATON

In the beginning there was food. The word came later, and when it did, food never seemed quite the same again. For the more fortunate among us, food, however pleasurable, is first regarded as a basic necessity that we take for granted as merely our due. Most specialists who are labeled "food writers" provide practical assistance with detailed hows and whys, but rarely do they add cultural, spiritual, or artistic dimensions to the mundane tasks of shopping, cooking, and cleaning up.

Far more valuable are the stories, novels, and essays of those I think of as "real" writers. Weaving food and the activities it engenders into the tapestries of the lives and events they portray, such writers put us in touch with our longings and lusts, our personal history and humanity, as they make us realize that bread is never bread alone.

The delicate sampling of such writing in this collection, and Laurie Rubin's elegant photographs that illustrate it, should satisfy even the finickiest literary appetite — and it offers a rich reward. For reading about food is the next best thing to eating it, and fortunately, is a lot less fattening.

Robert Benchley, for example, sparks memories of my own childhood treats with no danger of tooth decay, as he recalls "Yesterday's Sweetmeats," the penny candies of his day. "Colored Corrosion" he calls some, with as much affection as disdain, adding

■ I N T R O D U C T I O N ■

the tingling adventure of others that are at once "poisonous and delicious," as are so many of life's most irresistible temptations. Reading his account of "all-day-suckers," the big balls of hard candy that revealed different-color layers as they were consumed, I recall the sticky thrill of removing the candy from my mouth every few seconds to see what color I was up to.

Perhaps no piece evoked so personal a memory as Somerset Maugham's harrowing tale of a young man being led to financial slaughter by a woman who orders more food in a restaurant than he can pay for. "I never eat more than one thing," she assures him at the start. "Unless you have some caviar. I never mind caviar." It brought back all too clearly the sweaty terror I felt at the old Café Rouge in New York's Hotel Pennsylvania, where, as Tommy Dorsey's band played, I ordered so lavishly that my date had to leave his watch for collateral. His mother never forgave me.

A more touching if less familiar drama is played out in John Steinbeck's poignant story "Tortilla and Beans," in which a poor Mexican family thrives on that simple but sustaining diet, and discovers illness, malnutrition, and assorted troubles only when fed rich man's fare by well-meaning interlopers.

Strictly for the hungry imagination are the fey feastings at Sylvia Townsend Warner's court of Elfindom. There Ludla, a Merlin of a cook, daily proves "The Power of Cookery" with exhilarating eel soup, venison that has a texture both substantial and yielding, autumnally fragrant game pies, and beguiling apple strudel rivaled only by her brandied plums in marzipan jackets, until one day, alas, she is gone....

I N T R O D U C T I O N

There is more — much more — but none more headily passionate than Thomas Wolfe's accounts of the food markets and groaning board tables that serve a ravenous and discerning traveling circus crew. To Wolfe, obviously, as to so many of us, there is excitement in sheer abundance. Obtaining food is the task of a young boy halfway between childhood and manhood who shows a special talent for his work. Going to local country markets as soon as the caravan has pulled into towns, he seeks "country melons bedded in sweet hay…cool sweet prints of butter wrapped in clean wet clothes…cans foaming with fresh milk…limy pullets…," tomatoes heavy with red ripeness, apples with a powerful winy odor and "juicy corn stacked up in shocks of living green." Meals include potatoes "whipped to a creamy smother," boats swimming with pure beef gravy, breakfast steaks "hot from the pan and lashed with onions," and similar gustatory wonders that man indulged in so happily before the bluenose cholesterol watchers sauced our pleasures with guilt.

Finally, the circus route takes this boy to the long-sought home of his father and brothers, where, Wolfe writes, "They surrounded him with love and lavish heapings on his plate…," and we are reminded that food can be a manifestation of love, if indeed we need reminding. Finally, the boy is home and "filled with the strong joy of food, with the love of traveling and with danger and hard labor."

Who could ask for anything more?

ix
■

Yesterday's Sweetmeats

I T IS A RATHER DANGEROUS THING TO NOTE ENCOURaging tendencies in our national life, for just as soon as someone comes out with a statement that we are better than we used to be, we suddenly prance into another war, or a million people rush out and buy Crude Oil, preferred, or there is an epidemic of mother murders, and we are right back in the neolithic age again with our hair in our eyes.

But in the matter of children's candy I am afraid that we shall have to come right out and say definitely that the trend is upward. When I look back on the days of my youth and remember the candy that I used to impose on my stomach, the wonder is that I ever grew up to be the fine figure of a man that I now am. The wonder is that I ever grew up at all. Perhaps that was the idea, and I fooled them.

There were two distinct brands of candy in my day: the candy you bought in the drugstore on Sunday, when the candy shops were closed, and the weekday, or Colored Corrosion, brand, which, according to all present-day standards of pure food, should have set up a bright green fermentation, with electric lights, in the epiglottises of nine-tenths of the youth of that time.

ROBERT BENCHLEY

1

We can dismiss the Sunday drugstore candy with a word, for it was bought only once a week and then only for lack of something better. Its flavor was not enhanced by the fact that it was kept in tall glass jars, like appendixes, down at the end of the store where the prescriptions were filled, and consequently always had a faint suspicion of spirits of niter and sod. bicarb. about it.

The delicacy called "calves foot," for instance, which came in long ridged sticks, to be sucked with little or no relish, not only tasted of old French coffee on the second or third brewing, but gave you the undesirable feeling that it was also good for sore throat. The Sunday licorice sticks were larger and more unwieldy, and were definitely bitter on the tongue, besides costing a nickel apiece. Although the rock candy was sweet, it lacked any vestige of imagination in its makeup and made the eating of candy a hollow mockery, and, of course, horehound was frankly medicinal and could be employed only when everything else had failed.

It was on weekdays that the real orgy of poisoned and delicious candy took place, a dissipation which was to make a nation of dyspeptics of the present generation of businessmen and political leaders. This candy was usually bought in a little store run by an old lady (probably an agent in the employ of the German government, in a farsighted scheme to unfit the American people for participation in the war which was to come), and your arrival was heralded by the jangle of a bell not very cleverly concealed on the top of the door. This was followed by a long period of concentration, the prospective customer sliding his nose along the glass case from end to end, pausing only to ask the price of particularly attractive samples. The smell of those little candy shops is probably now a vanished scent of a bygone day, for it combined not only the aroma of old

candies and leather baseballs, but somehow the jangle of the little bell entered one's nostrils and titillated two senses at once.

In this collection of tasty morsels the one which haunts my memory most insistently is a confection called the "wine cup," a cone-shaped bit of colored sugar filled with some villainous fluid which, when bitten, ran down over the chin and onto the necktie. It was capped by a dingy piece of marshmallow which was supposed to be removed with the teeth before drinking the ambrosia within, but usually at the first nibble the whole structure collapsed, with the result that inveterate "wine-cup" consumers had a telltale coating of sugared water down the front of the coat, and, on a cold day, a slight glaze of ice on the chin. What went on in the stomach no one knows, but it does not make a very pretty picture for the imagination.

Another novelty was an imitation fried egg in a small frying pan, the whole sticky mess to be dug out with a little tin spoon which always bent double at the first application and had to be thrown away. The procedure from then on was to extract the so-called "egg" with the teeth, with chin jammed firmly into the lower part of the "frying pan" as a fulcrum. This, too, left its mark on the habitué, the smear sometimes extending as high up as the forehead if the nose was very small, as it usually was.

There was one invention which was fortunately short-lived, for even in those days of killers' candy it was a little too horrible for extended consumption. It consisted of two cubes (the forerunner of our bouillon cubes today) which, on being placed each in a glass of water and mixed with a soda-fountain technique, proceeded to effervesce with an ominous activity and form what was known either as "root beer," "ginger ale," or "strawberry soda," according to the color of the cubes.

The excitement of mixing them was hardly worth the distinct feeling of suicide which accompanied the drinking of the result, for God knows what they were or what the chemical formula for the precipitate could have been. Probably something which could have gone into the manufacture of a good, stable house paint or even guncotton.

The little mottoes, in the shape of tiny hearts, which carried such varied sentiments as "I Love You," "Skiddoo," "Kick Me," and "Kiss Me Quick," were probably harmless enough in their makeup, although I would always mistrust anything colored pink, but transporting them from shop to school and around the town loose in the pocket soon rendered them grimy and covered with gnirs (a "gnir" is a little particle of wool found in the bottom of pockets, especially constructed for adhering to candies) and unfit for anything involving an aesthetic sense.

"Chocolate babies" also made poor pocket candies, especially when in contact with "jelly beans." (The "jelly bean" seems to have survived down the ages and still is served in little bean pots from the original stock in the store. It would be interesting to discover why.) Licorice whips and "all-day suckers" (which changed color and design on being held in the mouth, a fact which seemed miraculous at the time, but which, on contemplation, sends a slight shudder down the middle-aged spine) were probably the safest of all early twentieth-century candies, but even they would probably fail miserably to pass the test of the Bureau of Standards at Washington.

Worst of all was the "prize package," a cone of old newspaper containing the odds and ends of the day's refuse — hard marshmallows with enough thumbprints on them to convict the candy dealer ten times over, quantities of tired popcorn which had

5
■

originally been pink, strange little oddments of green and red sugar which, even in their heyday, could not have been much, and, as the Prize, either a little piece of tin in the approximate shape of a horse or a button reading "Bust the Trusts." My gambling instinct made these "prize packages" a great favorite for my pennies, and it is to these and to old Mrs. Hill, who ran the candy shop and dispensed her largesse in this great-hearted manner, that I lay my present inability to eat eggs which have been boiled for more than eight seconds. Dear, *dear* Mrs. Hill!

And so, regardless of the present generation's freedom and reputed wildness, I will take a chance on their stomachs being in better shape at forty than mine is, for bootleg alcohol, whatever its drawbacks, takes away that craving for sweets which was the ruin of my generation.

✤

A Vicomte's Breakfast

HE VICOMTE DE V—— ONCE HAD BREAKFAST COSTING five hundred francs.

"A breakfast costing five hundred francs!" the reader will exclaim. "Why what ever do you mean; we fail to grasp the allusion."

Well, to explain; the Vicomte de V——, brother to Comte Horace de V——, and one of the most finished gourmets in France — and not only in France, but in Europe, not only in Europe, but in all the world — one day ventured to propound at a gathering, half artistic, half society, the startling statement —

"One man by himself can eat a dinner costing five hundred francs."

A universal shout of incredulity greeted the remark. "Impossible!" was heard on all sides.

"It is understood, of course," added the Vicomte, "that the word *eat* is taken to include the word *drink* as well."

"Why, of course."

"Well, then, I maintain that a man — and when I say a *man*, I do not mean a common yokel, you know, but a gourmet, a disciple of Montrond or Courchamp —

A L E X A N D R E   D U M A S

well. I say that a man, a gourmet of the sort I mean, is capable of eating a dinner costing five hundred francs."

"You could do it yourself, for instance?"

"Certainly I could."

"Will you wager you could?"

"By all means."

"I will hold the stakes," said one of the bystanders.

"Yes, and I will eat them," declared the Vicomte.

"Come, then, let us settle the details."

"It is all as simple as can be… I will dine at the Café de Paris, arrange my menu as I please, and consume five hundred francs' worth of dinner."

"Without leaving anything over in the dishes or on your plate?"

"Excuse me, I shall leave the bones."

"That is only fair."

"And when is the wager to be decided?"

"Tomorrow, if you like."

"Then, you won't eat any breakfast?"

"I shall breakfast just as usual."

"Well and good; for tomorrow, then, at seven o'clock, at the Café de Paris."

The same evening, the Vicomte de V—— went to dine as usual at the fashionable restaurant. Then, after the meal, so as not to be biased by any pangs of hunger, he set to work to draw up his menu for the following day.

The maître d'hôtel was summoned. It was midwinter. The Vicomte ordered

several kinds of fruit and spring vegetables, as well as game, which was out of season.

The maître d'hôtel demanded a week's delay to obtain these delicacies; and the dinner was accordingly postponed for that time.

To the right and left of the Vicomte's table the judges of the wager were to sit and dine. He was allowed two hours for the meal — from seven to nine. He might talk, or not, just as he pleased.

At the appointed hour the Vicomte walked in, bowed to the umpires, and took his seat.

The menu had been kept secret; the Vicomte's opponents were to be given the gratification of the unexpected.

When he was duly installed, twelve dozen Ostend oysters were set on the table, together with a half bottle of Johannisberg.

The Vicomte was in form; he called for a second gross of oysters and another half bottle of the same vintage.

Next came a tureen of swallows' nest soup, which the Vicomte poured into a bowl and drank off.

"Upon my word! gentlemen," he said, "I have a fine appetite today, and I feel greatly tempted to indulge a fancy."

"By all means! you are at liberty to do exactly as you like."

"I adore beefsteak and potatoes. — Here, waiter, a beefsteak and potatoes."

The man looked at the Vicomte in wonder.

"Well," added the latter, "don't you understand what I say?"

"Yes, sir, yes! but M. le Vicomte had settled his menu."

"True, true; but this is an extra, I will pay for it separately."

The umpires looked at one another. The dish was brought, and the Vicomte devoured it to the last scrap.

"Good!...and now the fish" — and the fish was set on the table.

"Gentlemen," observed the Vicomte, "it is a *ferra* from the Lake of Geneva, a fish only to be found there. Still it *can* be procured. I was shown it this morning as I sat at breakfast; it was then alive. It had been conveyed from Geneva to Paris swimming in lake water. I can recommend the dish; it is excellent."

Five minutes more and only the fish bones remained on the Vicomte's plate.

"The pheasant, waiter!" cried the Vicomte — and a truffled pheasant was duly served.

"Another bottle of Bordeaux, same vintage" — and the second bottle was produced.

The bird was disposed of in ten minutes.

"Monsieur," remarked the waiter at this point, "surely you have made a mistake in asking for the truffled pheasant before the stewed ortolans."

"Egad! but that's so. Luckily, it is not stipulated in what order the courses are to come; else I should have lost my bet. Now for the ortolans, waiter!"

There were ten, and the Vicomte made just ten mouthfuls of them.

"Gentlemen," said the Vicomte, "my menu is a very plain one now — asparagus, green peas, a pineapple, and a dish of strawberries. For wine — a half bottle of constantia, a half bottle of sherry, East Indian you know. Then, of course, to finish up with, the usual coffee and liqueurs."

11
∎

Each item appeared in due course — fruits and vegetables, all was eaten conscientiously, wines and liqueurs, all was drunk to the last drop.

The Vicomte had taken an hour and fourteen minutes over his dinner.

"Now, gentlemen," he said, turning to the umpires, "has everything been done honestly and aboveboard?"

The judges answered unanimously in the affirmative.

"Waiter, the bill!"

Observe, people did not use the word *addition* in those days, as they do now.

The Vicomte glanced at the total, and handed in the document to the judges.

It read as follows:

	Frs.
Ostend oysters, 24 dozen	30
Swallows' nest soup	150
Beefsteak and potatoes	2
Truffled pheasant	40
Stewed ortolans	50
Asparagus	15
Green peas	12
Pineapple	24
Strawberries	20
Wines and Liqueurs	
Johannisberg, one bottle	24
Bordeaux, best quality, 2 bottles	50

Constantia, half bottle 40

Sherry (East Indian), half bottle..................... 50

Coffee and liqueurs 1.50

_____

Total .... 580 Frs. .50

This total was duly verified and found correct.

This account was carried to the Vicomte's adversary, who was dining in a private room. In five minutes' time he appeared, bowed to the Vicomte, drew from his pocket six banknotes of a thousand francs, and handed them to him. This was the amount of the bet.

"Oh, sir," said the Vicomte, "there was no hurry about it; besides you would perhaps have liked to have your revenge."

"Should you feel inclined to give it to me, sir?"

"By all means."

"When?"

"Why," replied the Vicomte, with sublime simplicity, "now, at once, sir, if you wish."

The loser pondered deeply for a few seconds.

"Ah, no, upon my word!" he said at last; "after what I have seen, I think you are capable of anything."

The Luncheon

 CAUGHT SIGHT OF HER AT THE PLAY AND IN ANSWER to her beckoning I went over during the interval and sat down beside her. It was long since I had last seen her and if someone had not mentioned her name I hardly think I would have recognized her. She addressed me brightly.

"Well, it's many years since we first met. How time does fly! We're none of us getting any younger. Do you remember the first time I saw you? You asked me to luncheon."

Did I remember?

It was twenty years ago and I was living in Paris. I had a tiny apartment in the Latin Quarter overlooking a cemetery and I was earning barely enough money to keep body and soul together. She had read a book of mine and had written to me about it. I answered, thanking her, and presently I received from her another letter saying that she was passing through Paris and would like to have a chat with me; but her time was limited and the only free moment she had was on the following Thursday; she was spending the morning at the Luxembourg and would I give her a little luncheon at Foyot's afterwards? Foyot's is a restaurant at which the French senators eat and it was

W .   S O M E R S E T   M A U G H A M

15

so far beyond my means that I had never even thought of going there. But I was flattered and I was too young to have learned to say no to a woman. (Few men, I may add, learn this until they are too old to make it of any consequence to a woman what they say.) I had eighty francs (gold francs) to last me the rest of the month and a modest luncheon should not cost more than fifteen. If I cut out coffee for the next two weeks I could manage well enough.

I answered that I would meet my friend — by correspondence — at Foyot's on Thursday at half-past twelve. She was not so young as I expected and in appearance imposing rather than attractive. She was in fact a woman of forty (a charming age, but not one that excites a sudden and devastating passion at first sight), and she gave me the impression of having more teeth, white and large and even, than were necessary for any practical purpose. She was talkative, but since she seemed inclined to talk about me I was prepared to be an attentive listener.

I was startled when the bill of fare was brought, for the prices were a great deal higher than I had anticipated. But she reassured me.

"I never eat anything for luncheon," she said.

"Oh, don't say that!" I answered generously.

"I never eat more than one thing. I think people eat far too much nowadays. A little fish, perhaps. I wonder if they have any salmon."

Well, it was early in the year for salmon and it was not on the bill of fare, but I asked the waiter if there was any. Yes, a beautiful salmon had just come in, it was the first they had had. I ordered it for my guest. The waiter asked her if she would have something while it was being cooked.

"No," she answered, "I never eat more than one thing. Unless you have some caviar. I never mind caviar."

My heart sank a little. I knew I could not afford caviar, but I could not very well tell her that. I told the waiter by all means to bring caviar. For myself I chose the cheapest dish on the menu and that was a mutton chop.

"I think you're unwise to eat meat," she said. "I don't know how you can expect to work after eating heavy things like chops. I don't believe in overloading my stomach."

Then came the question of drink.

"I never drink anything for luncheon," she said.

"Neither do I," I answered promptly.

"Except white wine," she proceeded as though I had not spoken. "These French wines are so light. They're wonderful for the digestion."

"What would you like?" I asked, hospitable still, but not exactly effusive.

She gave me a bright and amicable flash of her white teeth.

"My doctor won't let me drink anything but champagne."

I fancy I turned a trifle pale. I ordered half a bottle. I mentioned casually that my doctor had absolutely forbidden me to drink champagne.

"What are you going to drink, then?"

"Water."

She ate the caviar and she ate the salmon. She talked gaily of art and literature and music. But I wondered what the bill would come to. When my mutton chop arrived she took me quite seriously to task.

"I see that you're in the habit of eating a heavy luncheon. I'm sure it's a mistake.

Why don't you follow my example and just eat one thing? I'm sure you'd feel ever so much better for it."

"I *am* only going to eat one thing," I said, as the waiter came again with the bill of fare.

She waved him aside with an airy gesture.

"No, no, I never eat anything for luncheon. Just a bite, I never want more than that, and I eat that more as an excuse for conversation than anything else. I couldn't possibly eat anything more — unless they had some of those giant asparagus. I should be sorry to leave Paris without having some of them."

My heart sank. I had seen them in the shops and I knew that they were horribly expensive. My mouth had often watered at the sight of them.

"Madame wants to know if you have any of those giant asparagus," I asked the waiter.

I tried with all my might to will him to say no. A happy smile spread over his broad, priest-like face, and he assured me that they had some so large, so splendid, so tender, that it was a marvel.

"I'm not in the least hungry," my guest sighed, "but if you insist I don't mind having some asparagus."

I ordered them.

"Aren't you going to have any?"

"No, I never eat asparagus."

"I know there are people who don't like them. The fact is, you ruin your palate by all the meat you eat."

19

■

We waited for the asparagus to be cooked. Panic seized me. It was not a question now how much money I should have left over for the rest of the month, but whether I had enough to pay the bill. It would be mortifying to find myself ten francs short and be obliged to borrow from my guest. I could not bring myself to do that. I knew exactly how much I had and if the bill came to more I made up my mind that I would put my hand in my pocket and with a dramatic cry start up and say it had been picked. Of course it would be awkward if she had not money enough either to pay the bill. Then the only thing would be to leave my watch and say I would come back and pay later.

The asparagus appeared. They were enormous, succulent and appetizing. The smell of the melted butter tickled my nostrils as the nostrils of Jehovah were tickled by the burnt offerings of the virtuous Semites. I watched the abandoned woman thrust them down her throat in large voluptuous mouthfuls and in my polite way I discoursed on the condition of the drama in the Balkans. At last she finished.

"Coffee?" I said.

"Yes, just an ice cream and coffee," she answered.

I was past caring now, so I ordered coffee for myself and an ice cream and coffee for her.

"You know, there's one thing I thoroughly believe in," she said, as she ate the ice cream. "One should always get up from a meal feeling one could eat a little more."

"Are you still hungry?" I asked faintly.

"Oh, no, I'm not hungry; you see, I don't eat luncheon. I have a cup of coffee in the morning and then dinner, but I never eat more than one thing for luncheon. I was speaking for you."

"Oh, I see!"

Then a terrible thing happened. While we were waiting for coffee, the headwaiter, with an ingratiating smile on his false face, came up to us bearing a large basket full of huge peaches. They had the blush of an innocent girl; they had the rich tone of an Italian landscape. But surely peaches were not in season then? Lord knew what they cost. I knew too — a little later, for my guest, going on with her conversation, absent-mindedly took one.

"You see, you've filled your stomach with a lot of meat" — my one miserable little chop — "and you can't eat any more. But I've just had a snack and I shall enjoy a peach."

The bill came and when I paid it I found that I had only enough for a quite inadequate tip. Her eyes rested for an instant on the three francs I left for the waiter and I knew that she thought me mean. But when I walked out of the restaurant I had the whole month before me and not a penny in my pocket.

"Follow my example," she said as we shook hands, "and never eat more than one thing at luncheon."

"I'll do better than that," I retorted. "I'll eat nothing for dinner tonight."

"Humorist!" she cried gaily, jumping into a cab. "You're quite a humorist!"

But I have had my revenge at last. I do not believe I am a vindictive man, but when the immortal gods take a hand in the matter it is pardonable to observe the result with complacency. Today she weighs three hundred pounds.

The Man Who Loved to Eat

NCE UPON A TIME THERE WAS A MAN WHO LOVED TO eat. Two helpings of this, a little more of that, and when he was full, out of consideration for his wife's feelings, he had a little more of something else. Half an hour after he had got up from the table, he would pass through the kitchen and, seeing the remains of the roast on its plat-ter, think regretfully, It won't be the same tomorrow. And then, after a guilty look over his shoulder, he would snitch a small piece of outside, not at all bothered by the fact that he was putting roast beef on top of the prune whip. Oddly enough, it did not occur to him that he was greedy until this was pointed out to him at a dinner party by the woman who sat on his left and who, for one reason and another, did not enjoy see-ing people eat. He thought a moment and then said, "Yes, it's true. I am greedy," and he decided to leave part of his dessert, but it was a particularly good strawberry mousse, and the next time he looked down, his plate was bare. He should have weighed three hundred pounds and waddled when he walked, but instead he was thin as a rail. He had always been thin. All that food did for him was keep up his appetite.

Though his wife ate sparingly, being mindful of her figure, she liked to cook for

WILLIAM MAXWELL

23

him, and his friends smiled as they watched him settle down to a menu. It is not moral perfection that most people find endearing but an agreeable mixture of strong points and frailties. His weakness was clearly the love of food, and he confidently expected to eat his way into his grave. But just when you think you know how things are going to be, it turns out that they aren't that way after all. "Will you have another helping of potatoes?" his wife asked one evening, and he started to say "Yes," as usual, and to his surprise he heard himself say "No." He had had enough. He couldn't eat any more, not even to please her. He wondered if he was coming down with something, and so, privately, did she.

The next morning he woke up feeling perfectly all right, and ate a huge breakfast, and that should have been the end of it, but there was a nagging doubt in the back of his mind: what happened once could happen again. He tried not to think about it. Four days later, when he sat down to the table, he found that once more he had no appetite. This time he was really frightened, and the nagging doubt moved from the back of his mind to the front, and stayed there. He ate, but out of the sense that it was something one must do. No real craving. At breakfast he did not find himself having just one more slice of buttered toast, with currant jelly on it because the other four slices had been either plain or with orange marmalade. He did not say, eyeing his wife's plate, "If that piece of bacon is going begging…" or "If you're not going to eat your English muffin…" He — who was never melancholy — caught himself out in a sigh, and asked himself questions that are better left unasked.

When it came time for his annual checkup, his doctor announced that his heart was normal and so was his blood pressure.

"You mean normal for my age," the man said gloomily.

"Yes. For a man of your age you're in very good shape. Appetite?"

"No appetite."

"Why not?"

"I don't know. I'm just not hungry. I'd just as soon never eat anything again as long as I live."

"We'll have to give you something for that," the doctor said, and he did. Though the man who loved to eat had absolute faith in any kind of medicine, and as a rule he showed marked signs of improvement before the pills or the antibiotic could possibly have had a chance to take effect, this time it was different. The liver shots did nothing whatever for him.

About once every month or six weeks his appetite would return, for no reason, and he would stuff himself and think, Ah, now it is over. I can go on eating...But the next time he sat down at the table, no sooner did he raise his fork to his mouth than with a look of utter misery he put it down again.

■ ■ ■

One day, passing by a secondhand bookstore, he happened to see, on a table of old, gritty, dehydrated books, the *Enchiridion* of Epictetus. He bought it and took it home and sat down to read it. "Require not things to happen as you wish, but wish them to happen as they do happen, and all will be well," Epictetus said, on page 8. The man who loved to eat took a pencil out of his inside coat pocket and underlined the sentence. A few pages farther on, he marked another: "Everything has two handles, the one by which it may be borne, the other by which it cannot." Suddenly he stopped reading and sat looking into space. The expression on his face was that of a person who had just been saved from drowning. "Umm," he said, to nobody in particular. He read on a few more pages, and then, having absorbed all the Stoicism he could manage in one dose, he closed the book and went about his business, thankful that his pleasure for food lasted as long as it did — though what is thankfulness compared to a good appetite?

✠

The Spoiled Cake

ME BORNET TORE OPEN THE TELEGRAM ALONG THE dotted line and read:

"CANNOT COME TONIGHT. INDISPOSED. REGARDS. LAFOY."

"How revolting!" she said. "*Indisposed!* I ask you, what kind of an excuse is that? After all my preparations."

"Such things only happen to us," said M. Bornet.

Mme Bornet reflected. "Now that I think of it, there is a solution. The Nolots are coming tomorrow. The cake will still be fresh. We can give it to them."

But next day, just as she was lighting the candles, she received a second telegram:

"IMPOSSIBLE FOR THIS EVENING. APOLOGIES. NOLOT."

"It's a conspiracy," said M. Bornet.

Livid and well-nigh prostrate, Mme Bornet could not bring herself to accept the relentlessness of fate. She opened her mouth wide to let the bitter words escape: "At nine o'clock they notify us. What ill-breeding!"

"Better late than never," said M. Bornet. "Anyway, you'd better calm down, old thing, or you'll curdle."

"Oh, you can laugh. It's a fine thing. This time the cake is really a total loss."

J U L E S   R E N A R D

"We'll have it for lunch tomorrow."

"If you think I buy cakes just for us to eat!…"

"No, of course not. But there's nothing else to do. We may as well resign our-selves."

"Very well," said Mme Bornet, "we'll throw our money out the window."

Vexed in her role as housewife, she spent a bad night, tossing and turning, while her husband slept very well, dreaming perhaps of vanilla frosting.

"He's looking forward to that cake," she thought.

As agreed, the maid, not without due precaution, brought in the cake at lunch. M. and Mme Bornet contemplated it. It had caved in, the cream had turned yellow and was seeping through the crevices, slowly submerging the eclairs. What had once resembled a fortified castle now recalled no known construction, at least not among those which are still standing. M. Bornet kept those observations to himself, and Mme Bornet began to cut the cake. Preoccupied with turning out equal portions, she said to her husband:

"You're making eyes at the bigger one. Pig!"

Her knife vanished beneath the flood of collapsing cream and scratched the plate, setting their teeth on edge. But she couldn't manage to establish limits, to trace dry pathways; the portions persisted in merging. Exasperated, she took the plate, spilled half the cake into her husband's dish, and said: "Here. Stuff yourself."

M. Bornet took a soup-spoonful, blowing upon it, for the cream had a very cold look. Then he thrust it into his mouth. But his tongue had its reservations and his lips refused to smack. He made a wry face, then grinned. "I think it's a little sour," he said.

"That's a good one," said madame. "Aren't we picky and choosy? My word, I don't know how to please you anymore. God in heaven, what did I do to deserve this?"

"You try it," said M. Bornet simply.

"There's no need for me to try it. I am sure in advance that it isn't in the least bit sour."

"Try it anyway. Just take one spoonful, just one."

"Two if you like," said Mme Bornet.

True to her word, she gulped them in quick succession and said: "See! There's nothing the matter with this cake. Oh, maybe it's a tiny bit ripe...."

But she took no more. She was on the point of tears when M. Bornet had an idea.

"Listen! You haven't given the concierge anything for a long time, and I've noticed that since New Year's Day his attentions have been falling off. Why not sacrifice ourselves? Let's give him the cake. We have a whole lifetime ahead of us to eat cake in."

"Well, at least put your share back," said Mme Bornet.

They sent for the the concierge. After the usual compliments M. Bornet held out the plate and said: "We should like to make you a present of this."

"You are too kind," said the concierge. "But won't you miss it?"

"No, no," said M. Bornet. "I've got it up to here." He pressed his Adam's apple and stuck out his tongue.

"Take it," said Mme Bornet. "Don't give it a thought. It's yours."

The concierge eyed the cake, sniffing ever so slightly, hesitated, then suddenly asked: "Has your cake got eggs in it?"

"Of course!" said M. Bornet. "You can't make a good cake without eggs."

"Then I'm very sorry. I don't like eggs."

"What are you telling him, my dear?" said Mme Bornet. "There's one egg yolk at the very most, just enough to bind the dough."

"Oh, madame, it makes me sick to my stomach just to hear a hen cluck."

"I assure you," said monsieur, "that the cake is exquisite. It will be a treat for you."

By way of proof, he dipped the tip of his finger into the cake and sucked it bravely.

"Maybe," said the concierge. "I wouldn't know. Anyway, I don't want it. I'd throw up. I beg your pardon and thank you just the same."

"But for your wife?"

"My wife is like me. She doesn't like eggs. She can't keep them down either. In a way, that's what brought us together."

"You could give it to your charming babies?"

"My kids? Oh, madame, the big one has trouble with his teeth, they've been falling out all over the place. Sweets are no good for him. And the little one, poor little fellow, isn't much of an eater yet."

"That's enough," said Mme Bornet coldly. "Let him be. We won't force you. We haven't the right. So sorry, my good man."

"Yes, it's quite enough," said M. Bornet in the tone he might have taken to repulse a beggar.

It was too humiliating. The concierge saw that they were displeased. Taken with scruples of delicacy, he did not wish to leave them with this unpleasant impression. "Monsieur," he said politely. "You are a scholar, you wouldn't happen to have a book with letters written in it, printed, you know, to wish somebody a happy name day, somebody called Honorine for instance? Now there's something that would give me pleasure and come in very handy. I'd bring it back."

They didn't so much as reply. Abashed, he retreated backward, feeling sure that he had offended them, and resolved to make up for his conduct by favors in his own province.

"Idiot!" said M. Bornet. "Why, those people are starving. Recently I saw their baby sucking a lettuce leaf."

"It was pride," said Mme Bornet. "You could see he was dying to take it."

She couldn't get over it. Her feverish fingers beat like little drumsticks on her temples. Elbows on table, monsieur studied one of his coat sleeves. No, really, it was too hard to find a taker for this cake. Pretty soon they would wash their hands of the whole thing.

"How stupid we are!" madame said at length, and sharply pressed the electric bell.

The maid appeared.

"Louise," said Mme Bornet crisply, "eat this. You will save your cheese for tomorrow."

Louise carried away the cake.

"She is certainly getting her fill of dessert. I can see her gobbling it up."

"It all depends," said monsieur. "I wouldn't be too sure. She's not the bumpkin she was, you know. Paris is making its mark. She's been wearing glass diamonds in her ears."

"I know. Ever since mistaken generosity made us take her to the circus, she's been juggling with the dishes. But she's not that refined. She's not going to be finicky when it's a question of her stomach."

"Eh, I've got my suspicions. She may bolt it down and she may not touch it."

"That is something I would like to see."

They waited; then, for one reason or another, Mme Bornet slipped quietly into the kitchen. She returned grinding her teeth with rage.

"Guess where our cake is now?"

M. Bornet reared up in his chair, swaying like a giant question mark.

"Guess. I'll give you a hundred guesses."

"Oh! I'm beginning to see red."

"In the garbage pail."

"That's too much!"

"Sacrifice yourself for strumpets like that. Lift them out of the gutter. There's your reward: 'Madame, I didn't come here to eat your rotten cakes!' But I call God to witness that she paid for her insolence."

Disdaining human speech, Mme Bornet held up the five fingers of her right hand and three fingers of her left hand.

"Eight days' notice," he muttered. "I should think so!" And his jowls grew leaden.

Face to face, they stirred one another to vengeance. She, holding up her eight fingers as though transfixed, felt the glow of her red ears, her inflamed forehead, her feverish cheeks, while his countenance grew blacker and blacker, like a window in the shadow of a slowly lowered awning.

Tortillas and Beans

EÑORA TERESINA CORTEZ AND HER EIGHT CHILDREN and her ancient mother lived in a pleasant cottage on the edge of the deep gulch that defines the southern frontier of Tortilla Flat. Teresina was a good figure of a mature woman, nearing thirty. Her mother, that ancient, dried, toothless one, relic of a past generation, was nearly fifty. It was long since anyone had remembered that her name was Angelica.

During the week work was ready to this vieja's hand, for it was her duty to feed, punish, cajole, dress and bed down seven of the eight children. Teresina was busy with the eighth, and with making certain preparations for the ninth.

On Sunday, however, the vieja, clad in black satin more ancient even than she, hatted in a grim and durable affair of black straw, on which were fastened two true cherries of enameled plaster, threw duty to the wind and went firmly to church, where she sat as motionless as the saints in their niches. Once a month, in the afternoon, she went to confession. It would be interesting to know what sins she confessed, and where she found the time to commit them, for in Teresina's house there were creepers,

JOHN STEINBECK

---

crawlers, stumblers, shriekers, cat-killers, fallers-out-of-trees; and each one of these charges could be trusted to be ravenous every two hours.

Is it any wonder that the vieja had a remote soul and nerves of steel? Any other kind would have gone screaming out of her body like little skyrockets.

Teresina was a mildly puzzled woman, as far as her mind was concerned. Her body was one of those perfect retorts for the distillation of children. The first baby, conceived when she was fourteen, had been a shock to her; such a shock, that she delivered it in the ball park at night, wrapped it in newspaper and left it for the night watchman to find. This is a secret. Even now Teresina might get into trouble if it were known.

When she was sixteen, Mr. Alfred Cortez married her and gave her his name and the two foundations of her family, Alfredo and Ernie. Mr. Cortez gave her that name gladly. He was only using it temporarily anyway. His name, before he came to Monterey and after he left, was Guglielmo. He went away after Ernie was born. Perhaps he foresaw that being married to Teresina was not going to be a quiet life.

The regularity with which she became a mother always astonished Teresina. It occurred sometimes that she could not remember who the father of the impending baby was; and occasionally she almost grew convinced that no lover was necessary. In the time when she had been under quarantine as a diphtheria carrier she conceived just the same. However, when a question became too complicated for her mind to unravel, she usually laid that problem in the arms of the Mother of Jesus, who, she knew, had more knowledge of, interest in and time for such things than she.

Teresina often went to confession. She was the despair of Father Ramon. Indeed

he had seen that while her knees, her hands and her lips did penance for an old sin, her modest and provocative eyes, flashing under drawn lashes, laid the foundations for a new one.

During the time I have been telling this, Teresina's ninth child was born, and for the moment she was unengaged. The vieja received another charge; Alfredo entered his third year in the first grade, Ernie his second, and Panchito went to school for the first time.

At about this time in California it became the stylish thing for school nurses to visit the classes and to catechize the children on intimate details of their home life. In the first grade, Alfredo was called into the principal's office, for it was thought that he looked thin.

The visiting nurse, trained in child psychology, said kindly, "Freddie, do you get enough to eat?"

"Sure," said Alfredo.

"Well, now. Tell me what you have for breakfast."

"Tortillas and beans," said Alfredo.

The nurse nodded her head dismally to the principal. "What do you have when you go home for lunch?"

"I don't go home."

"Don't you eat at noon?"

"Sure. I bring some beans wrapped up in a tortilla."

Actual alarm showed in the nurse's eyes, but she controlled herself. "At night what do you have to eat?"

"Tortillas and beans."

Her psychology deserted her. "Do you mean to stand there and tell me you eat nothing but tortillas and beans?"

Alfredo was astonished. "Jesus Christ," he said, "what more do you want?"

In due course the school doctor listened to the nurse's horrified report. One day he drove up to Teresina's house to look into the matter. As he walked through the yard the creepers, the crawlers and the stumblers were shrieking one terrible symphony. The doctor stood in the open kitchen door. With his own eyes he saw the vieja go to the stove, dip a great spoon into a kettle and sow the floor with boiled beans. Instantly the noise ceased. Creepers, crawlers and stumblers went to work with silent industry, moving from bean to bean, pausing only to eat them. The vieja went back to her chair for a few moments of peace. Under the bed, under the chairs, under the stove the children crawled with the intentness of little bugs. The doctor stayed two hours, for his scientific interest was piqued. He went away shaking his head.

He shook his head incredulously while he made his report. "I gave them every test I know of," he said, "teeth, skin, blood, skeleton, eyes, coordination. Gentlemen, they are living on what constitutes a slow poison, and they have from birth. Gentlemen, I tell you I have never seen healthier children in my life!" His emotion overcame him. "The little beasts," he cried. "I never saw such teeth in my life. I *never* saw such teeth!"

You will wonder how Teresina procured food for her family. When the bean threshers have passed, you will see, where they have stopped, big piles of bean chaff. If you will spread a blanket on the ground, and, on a windy afternoon, toss the chaff in the air over the blanket, you will understand that the threshers are not infallible.

For an afternoon of work you may collect twenty or more pounds of beans.

In the autumn the vieja and those children who could walk went into the fields and winnowed the chaff. The landowners did not mind, for she did no harm. It was a bad year when the vieja did not collect three or four hundred pounds of beans.

When you have four hundred pounds of beans in the house, you need have no fear of starvation. Other things, delicacies such as sugar, tomatoes, peppers, coffee, fish or meat may come sometimes miraculously, through the intercession of the Virgin, sometimes through industry or cleverness; but your beans are there, and you are safe. Beans are a roof over your stomach. Beans are a warm cloak against economic cold.

Only one thing could threaten the lives and happiness of the family of the Señora Teresina Cortez; that was a failure of the bean crop.

When the beans are ripe, the little bushes are pulled and gathered into piles, to dry crisp for the threshers. Then is the time to pray that the rain may hold off. When the little piles of beans lie in lines, yellow against the dark fields, you will see the farmers watching the sky, scowling with dread at every cloud that sails over; for if a rain comes, the bean piles must be turned over to dry again. And if more rain falls before they are dry, they must be turned again. If a third shower falls, mildew and rot set in, and the crop is lost.

When the beans were drying, it was vieja's custom to burn a candle to the Virgin.

In the year of which I speak, the beans were piled and the candle had been burned. At Teresina's house, the gunny sacks were laid out in readiness.

The threshing machines were oiled and cleaned.

A shower fell.

Extra hands rushed to the fields and turned the sodden hummocks of beans. The vieja burned another candle.

More rain fell.

Then the vieja bought two candles with a little gold piece she had kept for many years. The field hands turned over the beans to the sun again; and then came a downpour of cold streaking rain. Not a bean was harvested in all Monterey County. The soggy lumps were turned under by the plows.

Oh, then distress entered the house of Señora Teresina Cortez. The staff of life was broken; the little roof destroyed. Gone was that eternal verity, beans. At night the children cried with terror at the approaching starvation. They were not told, but they knew. The vieja sat in church, as always, but her lips drew back in a sneer when she looked at the Virgin. "You took my candles," she thought. "Ohee, yes. Greedy you are for candles. Oh, thoughtless one." And sullenly she transferred her allegiance to Santa Clara. She told Santa Clara of the injustice that had been done. She permitted herself a little malicious thought at the Virgin birth. "You know, sometimes Teresina can't remember either," she told Santa Clara viciously.

■ ■ ■

It has been said that Jesus Maria Corcoran was a great-hearted man. He had also that gift some humanitarians possess of being inevitably drawn toward those spheres where his instinct was needed. How many times had he not come upon young ladies when

they needed comforting. Toward any pain or sorrow he was irresistibly drawn. He had not been to Teresina's house for many months. If there is no mystical attraction between pain and humanitarianism, how did it happen that he went there to call on the very day when the last of the old year's beans was put in the pot?

He sat in Teresina's kitchen, gently brushing children off his legs. And he looked at Teresina with polite and pained eyes while she told of the calamity. He watched, fascinated, when she turned the last bean sack inside out to show that not one single bean was left. He nodded sympathetically when she pointed out the children, so soon to be skeletons, so soon to die of starvation.

Then the vieja told bitterly how she had been tricked by the Virgin. But upon this point, Jesus Maria was not sympathetic.

"What do you know, old one?" he said sternly. "Maybe the Blessed Virgin had business someplace else."

"But four candles I burned," the vieja insisted shrilly.

Jesus Maria regarded her coldly. "What are four candles to Her?" he said. "I have seen one church where She had hundreds. She is no miser of candles."

But his mind burned with Teresina's trouble. That evening he talked mightily and piteously to the friends at Danny's house. Out of his great heart he drew a compelling oratory, a passionate plea for those little children who had no beans. And so telling was his speech that the fire in his heart ignited the hearts of his friends. They leaped up. Their eyes glowed.

"The children shall not starve," they cried. "It shall be our trust!"

"We live in luxury," Pilon said.

"We shall give our substance," Danny agreed. "And if they needed a house, they could live here."

"Tomorrow we shall start," Pablo exclaimed. "No more laziness! To work! There are things to be done!"

Jesus Maria felt the gratification of a leader with followers.

Theirs was no idle boast. Fish they collected. The vegetable patch of the Hotel Del Monte they raided. It was a glorious game. Theft robbed of the stigma of theft, crime altruistically committed — What is more gratifying?

The Pirate raised the price of kindlings to thirty cents and went to three new restaurants every morning. Big Joe stole Mrs. Palochico's goat over and over again, and each time it went home.

Now food began to accumulate in the house of Teresina. Boxes of lettuce lay on her porch, spoiled mackerel filled the neighborhood with a strong odor. And still the flame of charity burned in the friends.

If you could see the complaint book at the Monterey Police Department, you would notice that during this time there was a minor crime wave in Monterey. The police car hurried from place to place. Here a chicken was taken, there a whole patch of pumpkins. Paladini Company reported the loss of two one-hundred-pound cases of abalone steaks.

Teresina's house was growing crowded. The kitchen was stacked high with food. The back porch overflowed with vegetables. Odors like those of a packing house permeated Tortilla Flat. Breathlessly the friends dashed about at their larcenies, and long they talked and planned with Teresina.

At first Teresina was maddened with joy at so much food, and her head was turned by the compliment. After a week of it, she was not so sure. The baby was down with colic, Ernie had some kind of bowel trouble, Alfredo's face was flushed. The creepers and crawlers cried all the time. Teresina was ashamed to tell the friends what she must tell them. It took her several days to get her courage up; and during that time there arrived fifty pounds of celery and a crate of cantaloupes. At last she had to tell them. The neighbors were beginning to look at her with lifted brows.

She asked all of Danny's friends into her kitchen, and then she informed them of the trouble, modestly and carefully, that their feelings might not be hurt.

"Green things and fruit are not good for children," she explained. "Milk is constipating to a baby after it is weaned." She pointed to the flushed and irritable children. See, they were all sick. They were not getting the proper food.

"What is the proper food?" Pilon demanded.

"Beans," she said. "There you have something to trust, something that will not go right through you."

The friends went silently away. They pretended to themselves to be disheartened, but they knew that the first fire of their enthusiasm had been lacking for several days.

At Danny's house they held a conference.

This must not be told in some circles, for the charge might be serious.

Long after midnight, four dark forms who shall be nameless, moved like shadows through the town. Four indistinct shapes crept up on the Western Warehouse Company platform. The watchman said, afterward, that he heard sounds, investigated and saw nothing. He could not say how the thing was done, how a lock was broken and the door forced. Only four men know that the watchman was sound asleep, and they will never tell on him.

A little later the four shadows left the warehouse, and now they were bent under tremendous loads. Pantings and snortings came from the shadows.

At three o'clock in the morning Teresina was awakened by hearing her back door open. "Who is there?" she cried.

There was no answer, but she heard four great thumps that shook the house. She lighted a candle and went to the kitchen in her bare feet. There, against the wall, stood four one-hundred-pound sacks of pink beans.

Teresina rushed in and awakened the vieja. "A miracle!" she cried. "Come look in the kitchen."

The vieja regarded with shame the plump full sacks. "Oh, miserable dirty sinner am I," she moaned. "Oh, Holy Mother, look with pity on an old fool. Every month thou shalt have a candle, as long as I live."

At Danny's house, four friends were lying happily in their blankets. What pillow can one have like a good conscience? They slept well into the afternoon, for their work was done.

And Teresina discovered, by a method she had found to be infallible, that she was going to have a baby. As she poured a quart of the new beans into the kettle, she wondered idly which one of Danny's friends was responsible.

The Power of Cookery

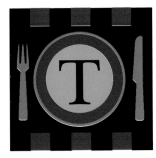

T HE SERVANTS' HALL AT SCHLOSS DREIVIERTELSTEIN — an Elfin court in Styria — was a Gothic apartment with an oriel window overlooking the poultry yard. At the head of the long table was a discarded throne, and there sat Ludla, the cook. In order of hierarchy, the throne should have been the housekeeper's, but Ludla's pre-eminence was indisputable, so the housekeeper sat at the other end of the table in a handsome chair of Spanish workmanship. At Ludla's right hand sat Ernolf, the butler; at her left, the cellarer, Gunf. The housekeeper was supported by the chief lady's maid and the head huntsman. Valets, footmen, grooms, housemaids, laundresses, etc., sat in ordered ranks on either side.

All these were working fairies, and their sleeping accommodation was poky. It was compensated for by their victuals. Their food was identical with the food served at the Queen's table — only hotter. Count Horn, the Royal Favorite, sometimes paused at the stairhead and sniffed wistfully. When Horn was young he was the soul of poetry and often forgot to eat. Many years had passed over him since. He retained his post (Queen Aigle was a traditionalist), but the poetry had waned to regretfulness and greed.

SYLVIA TOWNSEND WARNER

Ludla's cooking was renowned throughout Elfindom. Dreiviertelstein was an unimportant Kingdom, but to go on an embassy to Dreiviertelstein was something to be contested for, boasted of and ardently remembered. Nowhere else was stuffed goose such a fulfilling experience, eel soup so exhilarating, haunches of venison of such a texture, substantial yet yielding, game pies so autumnally fragrant, dumplings in such a variety of modest perfection, apple strudel so beguiling; though whether Ludla's brandied plums in marzipan jackets did or did not surpass her apple strudel was a pious debate.

Ambassadors timed their visits to coincide with Royal Birthdays, which were solemnized by Ludla's crawfish soufflé. The preparation for this fleeting delicacy began at dawn, when the crawfish were netted from the brook by teams of hardy scullions. They were plunged into precisely boiling water, and as they boiled, the Schloss cats set up an impassioned, visionary mewing. The flesh, freed from every fragment of shell, was gently, methodically pounded in marble mortars to a smooth paste by kitchen maids; cream skimmed from the wide bowls of overnight milk was added, while other kitchen maids whipped the whites of countless eggs. When all this was done to Ludla's satisfaction, and the ovens stoked to a steady heat, she did the flavoring. The flavoring was her secret. While she was at it, everyone was banished from the kitchen, and a holy silence settled on court life. It was of a crawfish soufflé that Count Luxus committed his only metaphor. "It is like eating a cloud," he said. His cousin Count Brock, who had a more searching mind, replied, "But, unlike a cloud, it nourishes."

The only person at Dreiviertelstein unmoved by Ludla's cooking was Queen Aigle. For her, meals recurred like sunrise and sunset. If a sauce had been curdled, a

dumpling petrified, she would have acknowledged its cometlike apparition without feeling personally involved.

Aigle was a High Romantic. She saw life as an occasion for achieving the improbable, for aiming at the unseen, and enforced this frame of mind on others. For the enforcing, she relied on quests. She could not go questing herself, being a Queen, or send her ladies on them, questing being unsuitable for ladies; and the working fairies already had their duties to carry out. But for the male half of her court she invented one quest after another. The quests necessarily complied with the seasons: in the winter months they were domesticated, their objects ranging from a lost thimble or the Absolute to a B flat in *alt.* With the spring, they soared. There was the Quest for the White Gentian, when the mountain slopes were speckled with stooping questers. There was the Quest for the Toad in a Stone, when the mountain peaks rang with the tap-tap of geological hammers and the curses of those whose hammers fell awry. There was the Quest for the Purple Carp, the Chamois Shod in Silver, the Ring Hung on the Topmost Bough, the Crested Hazel Hen. For several summers there had been a Quest of the Dragon, but this was abandoned, not so much because dragons were out-of-date as on account of so many questers being lost in caverns, some never to be found again. When Aigle's invention faltered, there was always the Quest of the Four-Leafed Clover to fall back on. There was also the twice-yearly competition for the First and Last Rose of Summer.

In the servants' hall opinions differed about the quests. The valets disapproved of them because of the clothes to be brushed and the boots polished, the housemaids because of the dirt tracked indoors. The kitchen fairies were sympathetic, and laid bets. Ludla invented a recipe for the Purple Carp, whose coloring she proposed to reinforce with beetroot. Meanwhile she put up picnic lunches.

The only valet who had no grounds for complaint was Prince Ingobaldo's. Ingobaldo was the Royal Consort, and felt it his duty to stay indoors to protect Aigle if the castle were struck by lightning. (Privately he wished it might be; he came from a Cisalpine Kingdom, and preferred a calmer style of architecture.) Marriage had brought him a severe disappointment. Pacing the distances and then measuring them with a wheel, he found that Dreiviertelstein was situated at five-eighths of the ascent from the valley to the mountain summit. Anxious not to condemn too hastily, he sought for a stone at the three-quarters mark. There wasn't one. But he had Ludla's cooking, perfection in an imperfect world; he had a quest of his own, an indoor quest for a sublime hour when his collection of striking clocks (five of them musical) would strike the hour simultaneously and the favorite melodies of Thuringia, Bohemia, the Veneto, Switzerland, and Capri mingle as one; and he enjoyed naming cats. There was no child of the marriage.

During the long summer hours when the questers were out, the elder court ladies slept, played cards, or wrote their memoirs; the young ones gathered sprigs of rosemary and bay, shook the insects out of them, and wove the daily garland with which Queen Aigle might crown whoever had achieved the current quest. The garland was seldom awarded. Every now and then, someone would find a four-leafed clover; the First and the Last Rose were reliable events. But though the White Gentian had been found and the garland bestowed, a cloud hung over the proceedings. The gentian was pallid, rather than white, and lacked the usual gentian stamina. There was a suspicion, though no one voiced it publicly, that its finder had blanched it artificially under an inverted flowerpot. The rosemaries and the bay trees grew in tubs along the South Terrace, and by the time they were brought in to winter in the conservatory, they looked impoverished, as they were also requisitioned by Ludla — the rosemary for roast pork, the bay leaves for game pies and custards. Like her Queen, Ludla was a traditionalist. A boar's head would have had no breath of the wild for her without a lemon between its jaws and celery whiskers.

Another summer was closing, the last of its Last Roses had been found, the last garland of the season given, and Aigle was inscribing this event in the Chronicle of Dreiviertelstein. The quality of the ink varied from time to time, but otherwise there was not much variation in the entries. A death, the first snowfall, a birth, an avalanche, an embassy...these were things to be expected. Everything in nature submits to becoming something to be expected. The hopes fastened on a new quest submit to the law of averages and fade. A stranger appears in an embassy, a traveling clockmaker stumbles through the snow and is sheltered for the night; they come again, and are no longer strangers. Schloss Dreiviertelstein was out of the way of interesting arrivals. The day of Wandering Minstrels, Tired Pilgrims, was over. In any case, these would probably be mortals, and as such irrelevant to a factual Elfin chronicle.

Even so, at that moment an interesting arrival, a seedy-looking young fairy, was circling over the castle and snuffing the air attentively.

His luck never failed him: it was a Michaelmas goose! He flew to a distance, alighted, closed his wings, and began to walk genteelly up the track. The plan of campaign formed in his mind. He would be mysterious, even a trifle standoffish. He would

not fall in love, or scratch himself, or talk with his mouth full. If the hospitality lived up to the promise of that smell, he would presently disclose that he had long known of the quests (which they had laughed about at the inn). He would hardly dare to ask if he, too… By the time he reached the castle, the plan was irreproachable. By the time he was within it, it was tossed away. Plans are an emcumberance. One does much better when prompted by truth and the moment.

That night Queen Aigle reopened the Chronicle and wrote the date, and beneath it: *Tamarind, Political Exile from the Kingdom of Tishk in the Ural Mountains.*

What charmed everyone was his frankness.

Exile is a discreditable term. Aigle had never imagined herself welcoming an exile; a political exile would presumably be someone even more skulking and hang-dog than the ordinary kind. Candor irradiated Tamarind's account of the situation at Tishk: the young Queen's power usurped by a militaristic uncle, the rising savagely put down, its leaders executed, their supporters exiled to beyond the Volga. No doubt such political rowdiness was typical of a Kingdom in the Urals. It was a greater effort of the imagination — few made it — to conceive the remoteness of Tishk. How long had the journey taken? How long had he traveled? For a moment, he hesitated. "Necessity knows no law. I must admit it. From time to time, I flew." And he described how he had flown over the Volga, so wide a river that he could not see its farther bank. There, on the farther bank, he lay exhausted, kissing the ground where every step would bring him nearer to Western civilization; and immediately had been set on by ignorant monks, who denounced him as a demon and handed him over to the police, who proposed to hang him as a spy. But one of them was venal and humane, and let him escape. "One has only to be in adversity," Tamarind exclaimed, gazing round on the table with his bright, rather bulging eyes, "to learn the good-heartedness of the poor and oppressed."

Aigle listened with her hands clenched in her lap and her mouth open. The clocks and the favorite airs had told midnight before anyone thought of going to bed.

Tamarind's frankness not only charmed his listeners; it infected them. They felt a compulsion to unbosom themselves to this unguaranteed exile from a Kingdom no one had heard of. They pursued him into corners and told him of doubts suppressed, smothered dissatisfactions, hopes strangled at birth, the true story — in time, several true stories — of the White Gentian; other true stories of machinations, favoritism, and neglected sunstroke; of lawsuits, armorial bearings, and little adjustments that would make the whole difference. The elder ladies read him their memoirs. Count Horn resurrected his juvenilia and recited them. Ingobaldo consulted him about the clocks.

When Tamarind could be persuaded to leave off talking himself, he was a sympathetic listener and an adept questioner. At the end of a week he was in an unsurpassed position to make mischief. But he had higher aims. Aigle, with her quests taken out of some worm-eaten tapestry, Aigle, stiff as her stays, a dedicated offering to old age, who listened, biting her lip like a virgin, Aigle, that withered child, had not unbosomed herself of a shred of confidence. His talent for understanding, for fellow-feeling, for reciprocation was wasted on her. It was mortifying. He could not make it out. Meanwhile, he played with real children — for there were children at Dreiviertelstein, though they seemed out of place there. They fastened on him as though he were food

55
∎

for the starving — they shouted, buffooned, rolled on the ground. He told them about good bears and bad bears, and of Baba Jaga the witch, who was, he said, his aunt. He also led them on a raid into the kitchen, where they stuffed themselves with candied violets and licked caramel off their fingers. Ludla officially disapproved, but if he had come without those distracting children she would have told him any secret he chose to ask, even the secret of the crawfish soufflé.

All this was hard to account for. He was ungainly and pasty-faced, his voice was harsh, he knocked things over, he had thick lips, his ears stuck out like an animal's; when he arrived his clothes were in tatters and he looked like a tramp. Ingobaldo supplied him with new clothes and an accomplished valet, and the result of this kindness was that he looked like a tramp who had pillaged a nobleman. Yet everyone liked him; even the working fairies liked him. He was lively, he was happy, and his happiness diffused like a scented oil. Every day confirmed Tamarind's belief in the good-heartedness of the poor and oppressed — for such he judged the courtiers of Dreiviertelstein to be.

And still their Queen eluded him.

She did not avoid him; she did not make even that acknowledgment of his zeal to release her deeper feelings.

It was her morning custom to take a brisk walk in the tiltyard. As usual, she was walking alone; as usual, he joined her; as usual, she hoped he had had a good night. The turf was lightly crisped with overnight frost. The air was scentless. The season's new-fallen snow glittered on the mountain peak. She stopped and looked at it. "How wonderful it must be, up there," she said. "How remote! How pure!"

Tamarind's luck stood at his elbow.

"Then let us fly there — this very minute."

"Fly? Fly? But I have never flown."

Was the poor lady malformed, or merely a slave to convention? He began to persuade. Flying was a delightful sensation, the easiest thing in the world, the most natural. It lifted one into an incomparable sense of freedom. There one is, with the world below one — a new world, seen from above. Today was an ideal day to take wing; the conditions could not be better.

As he spoke, she unclasped her mantle and let it slip to the ground. There were her wings. He had expected them to be puny; they were well developed, dove-colored, and shone.

"What beautiful wings!" he exclaimed. "And waiting all those years to be spread." The question was: Would they spread, or had they grown rigid in their folds? She shrugged. They quivered, unfolded smoothly, closed again, not so compactly.

"And so lustrous," he said.

"My bowerwomen oil them once a week, of course."

It was her first confidence. This indeed was Western civilization; no one at Tishk oiled his wings. Tamarind felt himself moving in a new world and perfectly at ease in it. He put his arm round Aigle's waist. "Allow me to support you for the first ascent. Trust yourself to me. Now!"

They rose in the air. She was heavier than he expected — women always are — and passive. He fixed his gaze on the mountain peak, tightened his grasp, and flew vigorously. He felt an erratic counter-rhythm, she wrenched herself free, lurched downward, recovered, and flew with the sudden brilliance of a beginner. He had to fly hard to catch up with her and set her on course again. She had no sense of direction; twice she collided with him. He seized her hand. Unless he could control her it would be impossible to make a safe landing — and the peak was now so near that he could feel its chill on his face. She jerked his hand away, flew vehemently ahead, plunged downward, too late and much too fast. She'll dash herself to pieces on the rock face, he thought, and shouted to her to slacken speed and veer to one side. Without slackening speed she made a violent turn, lost the rhythm of her flight, tumbled like a shot bird, just missed the rock, and landed head foremost in a lap of snow.

A flurry of snow hid her.

By the time he reached her she had righted herself and was sitting up, with blood dripping from her nose. No fairy likes the sight or smell of blood; life at Tishk had not reconciled Tamarind to its exhibition. He gave her his handkerchief and occupied himself with patting her back and examining her wings. One of them was slightly bent, and she winced as he touched it. He apologized politely and gloomily.

It was a situation where politeness had a shallow ring. Politeness would not quench Aigle's nosebleeding, or ward off the cold which was creeping into him from the snow, or ease the journey back (though it would almost certainly oblige him to carry her), or overcome the awkwardness of their return — for it was bound to be awkward, with a great many questions being asked and no attention paid to the answers. The fault lay in the unnaturalness of a society where the privileged classes debar themselves from their birthright of flying in order to assert a hereditary claim to go on foot, as though they were mortals. Mortals, meanwhile, long, like pigs in the proverb, for wings. It is not enough for them to admit the superiority of the Elfin race; they invent a flying species of mortal, and with the exaggeration of ignorance bestow wings in triplicate.

Aigle, earthbound at the summit of her social pyramid, sat beside him bleeding at the nose because she had never flown before, whereas if he had invited one of the working fairies — that fat old cook, for instance, Ludla or some such name — she would have flown like a bird, alighted like a feather. The unnaturalness of society was such a rich theme for meditation that he was startled when Aigle said that her nose had left off bleeding and they should think about getting back. He helped her onto her feet, he helped her into the air. From then on, she flew unaided. As they neared the castle she said they must separate. If her absence had been noticed, she would explain she had been looking for her mantle, which had somehow fallen off without her knowing it. He, too, had better have some excuse in readiness. She spoke coldly, and he could not help feeling snubbed. It was unfortunate she had got so overexcited; but he had given her a new experience, and should have received a word of thanks.

Within an hour of their return much of what had happened — and more that had not happened — was known in the servants' quarters, where the working fairies with one accord resumed their right and proper xenophobia. These Russians are all the same, wherever they come from. Tamarind himself had said his aunt was a witch. It was the old story — warm a serpent and he'll sting. Given new clothes, treated like a prince, allowed to wind the clocks even — and all the time casting a spell over Her Majesty. He wasn't a witch's nephew for nothing.... No, no! said others — she was not bewitched! When he grabbed her she fought and struggled for a good half hour; that

was when her mantle fell off — torn off, more likely. But all to no purpose, poor lady! Off he flew with her like an eagle with a lamb. And then to land his great fist on Her Majesty's nose — there's gratitude for you! No wonder she had a headache and had to lie down.

Ludla said she wished she could get after him with her rolling pin.

"It's a pity you can't poison him with your pie," said Ernolf, the butler. "I'd see to it he got the right helping."

For the main dish that evening was to be Ludla's Hunters' Pie — a standing pie like a fortress. Already she was stripping the flesh off the bones, breaking the carcasses and putting them in the great stewpan, where they would simmer down to a compounded broth of capercaillie, grouse, pheasant, partridge, woodcock, and hazel hens. The flesh lay on different platters, according to the time required for parcooking before it was enclosed in the fortress and the fortress went into the oven. A Hunters' Pie was a day's work, and the kitchen maids had been up since dawn, plucking and gutting. Pimentos, chanterelle mushrooms, garlic, juniper berries, segments of orange, anchovy fillets, dried and fresh herbs, salami that holds the mixture together, the grated chocolate that brings it to life were assembled; the flour had been sifted, the shortening flavored, reduced, and clarified. As the plan of battle lies in the general's brain, when to move the left wing, when to explode the mine, when to bring up the cavalry, so the plan of a Hunters' Pie and the obstacles chance might put in its way — a change in the wind upsetting the oven, an insufficiency of basil, the cat filching the anchovies — had occupied Ludla's mind since daybreak; and when she wished she could get at Tamarind with her rolling pin it was not so much the assault on the Queen she resented as the threat to the concentration demanded by the pie.

However, it was a splendid example of her skill and, preceded by a white soup and grilled trout, it entered the dining room like a conqueror. Only Aigle was unmoved. Her face was plastered with white lead, she wore her diamonds, and exuded a strong smell of Four Thieves vinegar. The animation roused by the pie's advent wasn't up to the usual mark; it flickered, and died out. An uneasy glumness settled on the company. Even Tamarind fell silent. He was hungry and the pie was absorbing. Count Horn was heard observing to Ingobaldo that he felt like sending a message of congratulation to the kitchen. "So do I, so do I," exclaimed Tamarind. "Let us send a fraternal greeting, an acknowledgment of our indebtedness. Food is an element in the interdependence of Elfins. Without cooks, we should be reduced to cannib —" His voice strangled in a gasp. He had swallowed too rapidly, something had stuck in his gullet, he had choked. Attention was politely averted. Ernolf came up unobtrusively with a napkin. Tamarind stiffened, glared, flapped his hands; his neighbors thumped his back. There was a piercing scream. Ernolf and the thumpers were thrust aside by Queen Aigle, who seized one of Tamarind's flapping hands, clasped it to her breast, and implored him to speak. "Say you're not dying. I can't bear it if you die. You're all I have, you're the light of my eyes, I can't exist without you. Tamarind, Tamarind, speak to me!"

Tamarind continued to choke. Tears ran down his cheeks. Aigle's Lady in Waiting, looking sternly in the opposite direction, pushed a bottle of strong smelling salts between them. Tamarind made a violent effort, swallowed convulsively, and said in a weak voice, "I swallowed a bone."

He made a better recovery than Aigle, who fell into hysterics and had to be carried away. The Hunters' Pie was removed. They ate the rest of the meal without knowing what they ate.

An injury to her nose had given the Queen a concussion; her mind was temporarily unhinged. That was the Court Physician's verdict, and everyone was relieved to hear it.

The next morning, a footman was sent to summon the housekeeper to the Queen's chamber. The housekeeper obeyed and was told to fetch the cook.

Aigle was sitting up in a wide bed, propped up by a great many pillows. Ludla had only seen her at a distance before. With her first glance, she knew that this was how a Queen in her bed should look.

"Are you the cook?" asked Aigle.

"Yes, Majesty," said Ludla and curtsied again.

"Last night there was a bone in the pie. I cannot have carelessness. You are dismissed."

As Ludla did not move, Aigle gestured to the housekeeper to take her away. It was a long way from the bedside to the door. In the doorway Ludla stopped.

"Majesty."

"Shush," whispered the housekeeper, who in her heart was sorry for the old servant. "Shush. You'll only waste your breath."

"Majesty. I have cooked for you and your Court and your household for more years than I can tell. It will be more years than I can tell before you have another such cook. Dreiviertelstein will be a poor place without me — a poor, dwindled, ill-fed, out-

of-the-way castle, with visitors as glad to leave it as fleas leaving a killed rabbit that has grown cold."

She curtsied again, with her disgraced head held high, and walked out, hauling the housekeeper after her.

In the kitchen a ham was gently boiling, the bread dough was rising under a cloth, a chopping knife lay among the vegetables she had been preparing for a julienne soup. She took off her apron and sat with folded hands while her belongings were packed by the head kitchen maid. With a groom to carry them, she took wing for her birthplace in the forest. Her parents were dead, but her brother still lived on there, a forester and a notorious poacher.

The ham was boiled to rags before anyone remembered to dish it up. The dumplings which accompanied it moved Count Luxus to another of his skyey metaphors: he said they were like thunderbolts. Ernolf the butler whispered to Ingobaldo that Ludla had gone to visit her brother. He had not the courage to admit the truth.

Ingobaldo was not one of those chivalrous persons who strangle their wives and stab their rivals; when he inquired after Tamarind's throat he had no *arrière-pensée* of cutting it. He had sustained another disappointment. For some time, he had thought that Aigle would be the better for a cicisbeo and considered importing one from Italy. When Tamarind arrived — dauntless, romantic, unfortunate through no fault of his own, a high-minded exile from an unknown Kingdom, everything that would appeal to Aigle — Ingobaldo felt that the ideal cicisbeo had been vouchsafed; or rather, the raw material for the ideal cicisbeo, since Tamarind was untutored in a cicisbeo's accomplishments. But he was willing, lofty in his sentiments, anxious to please; all that was necessary was that he should ripen. Unfortunately, the process of ripening had got out of hand. Aigle had ripened too soon. Apparently she was too highly strung to be soothed by a novice cicisbeo. Unsoothed, she would feel slighted, and the consequences could be very painful for Tamarind. For his own sake, he must be got rid of; and he, Ingobaldo, must assert himself and deal the blow. As Royal Consort, it was his duty. He wished it wasn't. Tamarind flew the Volga far too often, and the striking train of the Favorite Air from Thuringia had been out of order ever since he oiled and adjusted it, but he came from an outer world and Ingobaldo would miss him.

He allowed a few meals to elapse before regretting that Tamarind could no longer be detained from his project of touring Western Europe. After a start of surprise, Tamarind agreed he could not be detained — and seemed to welcome the thought. His plans were indefinite. He might fly the Channel and visit England. Wherever he went, he could be sure of the good-heartedness of the poor and oppressed.

He departed to a *bon-aller* of cannon, with a great many useful gifts and a newly lined purse, and after embracing everyone in reach. Aigle stood at a turret window, waving a red handkerchief. He took it to refer to the ultimate liberation of Tishk, and was much affected.

A day or two later, meals suddenly improved. Gunf and the head huntsman led a revolt, ousted the kitchen maids, and took over the cooking. Their repertory was limited, they cooked without imagination, they relied too heavily on pimentos and celery seed. But meals were faithful and punctual, and meat eaters found no fault with them. Aigle ate without comment, and ate rather more than usual. She was feeding on grief — a windy diet that demands reinforcing. Ingobaldo had been right after all. What

Aigle had needed was a cicisbeo — briefly. Henceforward she cherished an imperishable sorrow and a beautiful unresisting memory. Dead to the world, she had an object in life. She dressed in black, slept like a dormouse, with that sacred handkerchief he had lent her to bleed on under her pillow, dreamed of flying, woke to a breakfast tray and after the breakfast tray an inkpot. Since the entry of *"Tamarind, Political Exile"* she had written nothing more in the Chronicle. But there were a great many inviting blank pages, and she filled them with poems, elegiac or narrative. The elegies, neatly copied by the younger ladies, were given as parting presents to the reluctant embassies that came to Dreiviertelstein — and left very much as Ludla had said they would.

There were no more quests. Her life was too full for quests.

Failing quests, it became the fashion to go for woodland walks. By twos and threes, by sixes and sevens, the woodland walkers, some with walking sticks, some with guns, and equipped with simple luncheons — a ham sandwich, a hard-boiled egg with lettuce — set out soon after breakfast. A couple of hours' walking brought them to Ludla's cottage home with a healthy appetite. There they would sit on the wooden benches outside the door, hearing Ludla pound and chop and stir, breathing up the dear familiar smells escaping when a saucepan lid was raised, an oven door opened. There they would sit, pious as pilgrims, sure of their faith's reward, hearing the forest rustle, and Ludla whisking eggs. And then there would be a clatter of plates and cutlery, and Ludla would come to the door and say, "You can come in now." As she had fewer to cook for, she cooked more lavishly. Her charges (which included second helpings) were moderate, and she spent part of her profits on the enhancements and delicacies she had commanded at the Schloss. Her only stipulation was that they should bring their wine.

His Father's Earth

A S THE BOY STOOD LOOKING AT THE CIRCUS WITH HIS brother, there came to him two images, which had haunted his childhood and the life of every boy who ever lived, but were now for the first time seen together with an instant and magic congruence. And these two images were of the circus and his father's earth.

He thought then he had joined a circus and started on the great tour of the nation with it. It was spring: the circus had started in New England and worked westward and then southward as the summer and autumn came on. His nominal duties — for, in his vision, every incident, each face and voice and circumstance were blazing real as life itself — were those of ticket seller, but in this tiny show, everyone did several things: the performers helped put up and take down the tents, load and unload the wagons, and the roustabouts and business people worked wherever they were needed.

The boy sold tickets, but he also posted bills and bartered with tradesmen and farmers in new places for fresh food. He became very shrewd and clever at this work, and loved to do it — some old, sharp, buried talent for shrewd trading, that had come to him from his mountain blood, now aided him. He could get the finest, freshest

T H O M A S   W O L F E

meats and vegetables at the lowest prices. The circus people were tough and hard, they always had a fierce and ravenous hunger, they would not accept bad food and cooking, they fed stupendously, and they always had the best of everything.

Usually the circus would arrive at a new town very early in the morning, before daybreak. He would go into town immediately: he would go to the markets, or with farmers who had come in for the circus. He felt and saw the purity of first light, he heard the sweet and sudden lutings of first birds, and suddenly he was filled with the earth and morning in new towns, among new men: he walked among the farmers' wagons, and dealt with them on the spot for the prodigal plenty of their wares — the country melons bedded in sweet hay of wagons, the cool sweet prints of butter wrapped in clean wet cloths, with dew and starlight still on them, the enormous battered cans foaming with fresh milk, the new laid eggs which he bought by the gross and hundred dozens, the tender limy pullets by the score, the rude country wagons laden to the rim with heaped abundancies — with delicate bunches of green scallions, the heavy red ripeness of huge tomatoes, the sweet-leaved lettuces crisp as celery, the fresh podded peas and the succulent young beans, as well as the potatoes spotted with the loamy earth, the powerful winey odor of the apples, the peaches, and the cherries, the juicy corn stacked up in shocks of living green, and the heavy blackened rinds of home-cured hams and bacons.

As the market opened, he would begin to trade and dicker with the butchers for their finest cuts of meat: they would hold great roasts up in their gouted fingers, they would roll up tubs of fresh ground sausage, they would smack with their long palms the flanks of beeves and porks: he would drive back to the circus with a wagon full of meat and vegetables.

At the circus ground the people were already in full activity. He could hear the wonderful timed tattoo of sledges on driven stakes, the shouts of men riding animals down to water, the slow clank and pull of mighty horses, the heavy rumble of the wagons as they rolled down off the circus flatcars. By now the eating table would be erected, and as he arrived, he could see the cooks already busy at their ranges, the long tables set up underneath the canvas with their rows of benches, their tin plates and cups, their strong readiness. There would be the amber indescribable pungency of strong coffee, and the smell of buckwheat batter.

And the circus people would come in for their breakfast: hard and tough, for the most part decent and serious people, the performers, the men and women, the acrobats, the riders, the tumblers, the clowns, the jugglers, the contortionists, and the balancers would come in quietly and eat with a savage and inspired intentness.

The food they ate was as masculine and fragrant as the world they dwelt in: it belonged to the stained world of mellow sun-warmed canvas, the clean and healthful odor of the animals, and the mild sweet lyric nature of the land in which they lived as wanderers, and it was there for the asking with a fabulous and stupefying plenty, golden and embrowned: they ate stacks of buckwheat cakes, smoking hot, soaked in hunks of yellow butter which they carved at will with a wide free gesture from the piled prints on the table, and which they garnished (if they pleased) with ropes of heavy black molasses, or with the lighter, freer maple syrup.

They ate big steaks for breakfast, hot from the pan and lashed with onions, they ate whole melons, crammed with the ripeness of the deep pink meat, rashers of bacon, and great platters of fried eggs, or eggs scrambled with calves' brains, they helped themselves from pyramids of fruit piled up at intervals on the table — plums, peaches, apples, cherries, grapes, oranges, and bananas — they had great pitchers of thick cream to pour on everything, and they washed their hunger down with pint mugs of strong deep-savored coffee.

For their midday meal they would eat fiercely, hungrily, with wolfish gusts, mightily, with knit brows and convulsive movements of their corded throats. They would eat great roasts of beef with crackled hides, browned in their juices, rare and tender, hot chunks of delicate pork with hems of fragrant fat, delicate young boiled chickens, only a mouthful for these ravenous jaws, twelve-pound pot roasts cooked for hours in an iron pot with new carrots, onions, sprouts, and young potatoes, together with every vegetable that the season yielded: huge roasting ears of corn, smoking hot, stacked like cord wood on two-foot platters, tomatoes cut in slabs with wedges of okra and succotash, and raw onion, mashed potatoes whipped to a creamy smother, boats swimming with pure beef gravy, new carrots, turnips, fresh peas cooked in butter, and fat string beans seasoned with the flavor of big chunks of cooking-pork. In addition, they had every fruit the place and time afforded: hot crusty apple, peach and cherry pies, encrusted with cinnamon, puddings and cakes of every sort, and blobbering cobblers inches deep.

Thus the circus moved across America, from town to town, from state to state, eating its way from Maine into the great plains of the West, eating its way along the Hudson and the Mississippi rivers, eating its way across the flat farm lands of the Pennsylvania Dutch colony, the eastern shore of Maryland and back again across the states of Virginia, North Carolina, Tennessee, and Florida — eating all good things that this

73
∎

enormous, this inevitably bountiful and abundant cornucopia of a continent yielded.

They ate the cod, bass, mackerel, halibut, clams, and oysters of the New England coast, the terrapin of Maryland, the fat beeves, porks, and cereals of the Middle West, and they had, as well, the heavy juicy peaches, watermelons, cantaloupes of Georgia, the fat sweet shad of the Carolina coasts, and the rounded and exotic citrus fruits of the tropics: the oranges, tangerines, bananas, kumquats, lemons, guavas down in Florida, together with a hundred other fruits and meats — the Vermont turkeys, the mountain trout, the bunched heaviness of the Concord grapes, the red winey bulk of the Oregon apples, as well as the clawed, shelled, and crusted dainties, the crabs, the clams, the pink meated lobsters that grope their way along the sea-floors of America.

The boy awoke at morning in three hundred towns with the glimmer of starlight on his face; he was the moon's man; then he saw light quicken in the east, he saw the pale stars drown, he saw the birth of light, he heard the lark's wing, the bird tree, the first liquorous liquefied lutings, the ripe-aired trillings, the plumskinned birdnotes, and he heard the hoof and wheel come down the streets of the nation. He exulted in his work as food-producer for the circus people, and they loved him for it. They said there had never been anyone like him — they banqueted exultantly, with hoarse gulpings and with joy, and they loved him.

Slowly, day by day, the circus worked its way across America, through forty states and through a dozen weathers. It was a little world that moved across the enormous loneliness of the earth, a little world that each day began a new life in new cities, and left nothing to betray where it had been save a litter of beaten papers, the droppings of the camel and the elephant in Illinois, a patch of trampled grass, and a magical memory.

The circus men knew no other earth but this; the earth came to them with the smell of canvas and the lion's roar. They saw the world behind the lights of the carnival, and everything beyond these lights was phantasmal and unreal to them; it lived for them within the circle of the tent as men and women who sat on benches, as the posts they came to, and sometimes as the enemy.

Their life was filled with the strong joy of food, with the love of traveling, and with danger and hard labor. Always there was the swift violence of change and movement, of putting up and tearing down, and sometimes there was the misery of rain and sleet, and mud above the ankles, of wind that shook their flimsy residence, that ripped the tent stakes from their moorings in the earth and lifted out the great center pole as if it were a match. Now they must wrestle with the wind and hold their dwelling to the earth; now they must fight the weariness of the mud and push their heavy wagons through the slime; now, cold and wet and wretched, they must sleep on piles of canvas, upon the flatcars in a driving rain, and sometimes they must fight the enemy — the drunk, the savage, the violent enemy, the bloody man, who dwelt in every place. Sometimes it was the city thug, sometimes the mill hands of the South, sometimes the miners in a Pennsylvania town — the circus people cried, "Hey, Rube!" and fought them with fist and foot, with pike and stake, and the boy saw and knew it all.

When the men in a little town barricaded the street against their parade, they charged the barricade with their animals, and once the sheriff tried to stop the elephant by saying: "Now, damn ye, if you stick your Goddamned trunk another inch, I'll shoot."

The circus moved across America foot by foot, mile by mile. He came to know the land. It was rooted in his blood and his brain forever — its food, its fruit, its fields and forests, its deserts, and its mountains, its savage lawlessness. He saw the crimes and the violence of the people with pity, with mercy, and with tenderness: he thought of them as if they were children. They smashed their neighbors' brains out with an ax, they disemboweled one another with knives, they were murderous and lost upon this earth they dwelt upon as strangers.

The tongueless blood of the murdered men ran down into the earth, and the earth received it. Upon the enormous and indifferent earth the little trains rattled on over ill-joined rails that loosely bound the sprawling little towns together. Lost and lonely, brief sawings of wood and plaster and cheap brick ugliness, the little towns were scattered like encampments through the wilderness. Only the earth remained, which all these people had barely touched, which all these people dwelt upon but could not possess.

Only the earth remained, the savage and lyrical earth with its rude potency, its thousand vistas, its heights and slopes and levels, with all its violence and delicacy, the terrible fecundity, decay, and growth, its fierce colors, its vital bite and sparkle, its exultancy of space and wandering. And the memory of this earth, the memory of all this universe of sight and sense, was rooted in this boy's heart and brain forever. It fed the hungers of desire and wandering, it breached the walls of his secret and withdrawn spirit. And for every memory of place and continent, of enormous coffee-colored rivers and eight hundred miles of bending wheat, of Atlantic coast and midland prairie, of raw red Piedmont and tropic flatness, there was always the small, fecund, perfect memory of his father's land, the dark side of his soul and his heart's desire, which he had never seen, but which he knew with every atom of his life, the strange phantasmal haunting of man's memory. It was a fertile, nobly swelling land, and it was large enough to live in, walled with fulfilled desire.

Abroad in this ocean of earth and vision he thought of his father's land, of its great red barns and nobly swelling earth, its clear familiarity and its haunting strangeness, and its dark and secret heart, its magnificent, its lovely and tragic beauty. He thought of its smell of harbors and its rumors of the seas, the city, and the ships, its wine-red apples and its brown-red soil, its snug weathered houses, and its lyric unutterable ecstasy.

A wonderful thing happened. One morning he awoke suddenly to find himself staring straight up at the pulsing splendor of the stars. At first he did not know where he was, but he knew instantly, even before he looked about him, that he had visited this place before. The circus train had stopped in the heart of the country, for what reason he did not know. He could hear the languid and intermittent breathing of the engine, the strangeness of men's voices in the dark, the casual stamp of the horses in their cars, and all around him the attentive and vital silence of the earth.

Suddenly he raised himself from the pile of canvas on which he slept. It was the moment just before dawn: against the east, the sky had already begun to whiten with the first faint luminosity of day, the invading tides of light crept up the sky, drowning the stars out as they went. The train had halted by a little river which ran swift and deep next to the tracks, and now he knew that what at first had been the sound of silence was the swift and ceaseless music of the river.

There had been rain the night before, and now the river was filled with the sweet

clean rain-drenched smell of earthy deposits. He could see the delicate white glimmer of young birch trees leaning from the banks, and on the other side he saw the winding whiteness of the road. Beyond the road, and bordering it, there was an orchard with a wall of lichened stone: a row of apple trees, gnarled and sweet, spread their squat twisted branches out across the road, and in the faint light he saw that they were dense with blossoms: the cool intoxication of their fragrance overpowered him.

As the wan light grew, the earth and all its contours emerged sharply, and he saw again the spare, gaunt loneliness of the earth at dawn, with all its sweet and sudden cries of spring. He saw the worn and ancient design of lichened rocks, the fertile soil of the baked fields, he saw the kept order, the frugal cleanliness, with its springtime overgrowth, the mild tang of opulent greenery. There was an earth with fences, as big as a man's heart, but not so great as his desire, and after his giant wanderings over the prodigal fecundity of the continent, the earth was like a room he once had lived in. He returned to it as a sailor to a small closed harbor, as a man, spent with the hunger of his wandering, comes home.

Instantly he recognized the scene. He knew that he had come at last into his father's land. It was magic that he knew but could not speak; he stood upon the lip of time, and all his life now seemed the mirage of some wizard's spell — the spell of canvas and the circus ring, the spell of the tented world which had possessed him. Here was his home, brought back to him while he slept, like a forgotten dream. Here was the dark side of his soul, his heart's desire, his father's country, the earth his spirit dwelt on as a child. He knew every inch of the landscape, and he knew, past reason, doubt, or argument, that home was not three miles away.

He got up at once and leaped down to the earth; he knew where he would go. Along the track there was a slow swing and dance of the brakemen's lamps, that moving, mournful, and beautiful cloud of light along the rails of the earth, that he had seen so many times. Already the train was in motion; its bell tolled and its heavy trucks rumbled away from him. He began to walk back along the tracks, for less than a mile away, he knew, where the stream boiled over the lip of the dam, there was a bridge. When he reached the bridge, a deeper light had come: the old red brick of the mill emerged sharply and with the tone and temper of deep joy fell sheer into bright shining waters.

He crossed the bridge and turned left along the road: here it moved away from the river, among fields and through dark woods — dark woods bordered with stark poignancy of fir and pine, with the noble spread of maples, shot with the naked whiteness of birch. Here was the woodland maze: the sweet density of the brake and growth. Sharp thrummings, woodland flitters broke the silence. His steps grew slow, he sat upon a wall, he waited.

Now rose the birdsong in first light, suddenly he heard each sound the birdsong made. Like a flight of shot the sharp fast skaps of sound arose. With chittering bicker, fast-fluttering skirrs of sound, the palmy honeyed bird-cries came. Smooth drops and nuggets of bright gold they were. Now sang the birdtrees filled with lutings in bright air: the thrums, the lark's wing, and tongue-trilling chirrs arose now. The little nameless cries arose and fell with liquorous liquified lutings, with lirruping chirp, plumbellied smoothness, sweet lucidity.

And now there was the rapid kweet kweet kweet kweet kweet of homing birds and

81
■

their pwee pwee pwee: others with sharp cricketing stitch, a mosquito buzz with thin metallic tongues, while some with rusty creakings, high shrew's caws, with eerie rasp, with harsh far calls — all birds that are awake in the sweet woodland tangles: and above, there passed the whirr of hidden wings, the strange lost cry of the unknown birds, in full flight now, in which the sweet confusion of their cries was mingled.

Then he got up and went along the road where, he knew, like the prophetic surmise of a dream, the house of his father's blood and kin lay hidden. At length, he came around a bending in the road, he left the wooded land, he passed by hedges and saw the old white house, set in the shoulder of the hill, worn like care and habit in the earth; clean and cool, it sat below the clean dark shelter of its trees: a twist of morning smoke coiled through its chimney.

Then he turned in to the rutted road that led up to the house, and at this moment the enormous figure of a powerful old man appeared around the corner prophetically bearing a smoked ham in one huge hand. And when the boy saw the old man, a cry of greeting burst from his throat, and the old man answered with a roar of welcome that shook the earth.

The old man dropped his ham, and waddled forward to meet the boy: they met half down the road, and the old man crushed him in his hug; they tried to speak but could not; they embraced again and in an instant all the years of wandering, the pain of loneliness and the fierce hungers of desire, were scoured away like a scum of frost from a bright glass.

He was a child again, he was a child that had stood upon the lip and leaf of time and heard the quiet tides that move us to our death, and he knew that the child could

not be born again, the book of days could never be turned back, old errors and confusions never righted. And he wept with sorrow for all that was lost and could never be regained, and with joy for all that had been recovered.

Suddenly he saw his youth as men on hilltops might look at the whole winding course of rivers to the sea, he saw the blind confusions of his wanderings across the earth, the horror of man's little stricken mote of earth against immensity, and he remembered the proud exultancy of his childhood when all the world lay like a coin between his palms, when he could have touched the horned rim of the moon, when heroes and great actions bent before him.

And he wept, not for himself, but out of love and pity for every youth that ever hoped and wandered and was alone. He had become a man, and he had in him unique glory that belongs to men alone, and that makes them great, and from which they shape their mightiest songs and legends. For out of their pain they utter first a cry for wounded self, then, as their vision deepens, widens, the universe of their marvelous sense leaps out and grips the universe; they feel contempt for gods, respect for men alone, and with the indifference of a selfless passion, enact earth out of a lyric cry.

At this moment, also, two young men burst from the house and came running down the road to greet him. They were powerful and heavy young men, already beginning to show signs of that epic and sensual grossness that distinguished their father. Like their father, they recognized the boy instantly, and in a moment he was engulfed in their mighty energies, borne up among them to the house. And they understood all he wanted to say, but could not speak, and they surrounded him with love and lavish heapings of his plate. And the boy knew the strange miracle of return to the dark land of his heart's desire, the father's land which haunts men like a dream they never knew.

Such were the twin images of the circus and his father's land which were to haunt his dreams and waking memory and which now, as he stood there with his brother looking at the circus, fused instantly to a living whole and came to him in a blaze of light.

And in this way, before he had ever set foot upon it, he came for the first time to his father's earth.

✛

C O N T R I B U T O R S

ROBERT BENCHLEY (1889–1945), the high-spirited knight of the Algonquin Roundtable set, was a natural-born humorist. He gained national celebrity as a radio and film star, winning an Academy Award in 1935 for his short film, "How to Sleep." He is best remembered for his books, *Twenty Thousand Leagues Under the Sea; or, David Copperfield* and *My Ten Years in a Quandary, and How It Grew.* "Yesterday's Sweetmeats" was written in 1932.

ALEXANDRE DUMAS (1802–1870), author of the swashbuckling classics *The Three Musketeers, The Count of Monte Cristo,* and *The Man in the Iron Mask,* was himself a master swordsman, crack marksman, soldier of fortune, and legendary Don Juan. Drawing from his own real-life escapades in the King's guard, his marvelous characters and their heroic adventures seem as real today as they were more than a century ago. "The Vicomte's Breakfast" was written circa 1830.

W. SOMERSET MAUGHAM (1874–1965), the author of hundreds of literary works, was one of the world's most commercially successful authors. In his lifetime he amassed a huge fortune earned from the sale of his bestselling books and long-running plays. He is best known for his novels, *Of Human Bondage, The Moon and Sixpence, Ashenden, Cakes and Ale,* and *The Razor's Edge,* all of which were later adapted for the stage or the screen. "The Luncheon" was first published in 1936.

86
■

WILLIAM MAXWELL (1908–) is the highly praised author of eleven novels and several works of non-fiction. He was a valued member of the editorial staff and a featured contributor at *New Yorker* magazine from 1936 to 1976. Although he is probably best known for his wonderful pieces in the *New Yorker,* two of his novels have been singled out as modern classics — *They Came Like Swallows* and *The Folded Leaf.* "The Man Who Loved to Eat" was published in 1966.

JULES RENARD (1864–1910) earned his keep as an educator, government official, publisher, tutor, ghostwriter, novelist, and playwright, gathering material for his novels and short stories along the way. Renard's disturbing and controversial autobiographical novel of a boy's stark childhood, *Poil de Carotte* [*Carrot Top*], is a French classic, exerting a powerful influence on modern French novelists. "The Spoiled Cake" was written circa 1900.

JOHN STEINBECK (1900–1968) is considered to be one of America's greatest writers. *The Grapes of Wrath, Tortilla Flat, Of Mice and Men, The Moon Is Down, East of Eden,* and the novel-length short-story collection, *The Long Valley,* are his literary legacy to the world. "Tortillas and Beans" was written in 1935.

SYLVIA TOWNSEND WARNER (1893–1978), illustrious British novelist, poet, translator, biographer, and editor, is probably best known for her lively short works of fantasy fiction that appeared with welcome frequency in *New Yorker* magazine. "The Power of Cookery" is one such story, published under the title "The Politics of Exile" in 1976.

THOMAS WOLFE (1900–1938) had an untimely death, sadly cutting short his brilliant career. Even so, he lived to see his two very long and revealing novels, *Look Homeward Angel* and *Of Time and the River,* become bestsellers. *The Web and the Rock, You Can't Go Home Again,* and *The Hills Beyond,* published after his death, were compiled and shaped by his editors from an eight-foot pile of manuscript that this prolific writer had left behind. "His Father's Earth" was published in 1939.